The Glastonbury Tales

J Lee Amey

GRANVILLE HOUSE

This is a work of fiction. Any similarities to actual persons, living or dead, or actual events, is purely coincidental.

This book is neither endorsed by, nor affiliated to, the Glastonbury Festival.

Copyright © J Lee Amey, 2024

All rights reserved. No reproduction, copy or transmission of this publication may be made without written permission. No paragraph of this publication may be reproduced, copied or transmitted save with written permission or in accordance with the provisions of the Copyright Act 1956 (as amended). Any person who does any unauthorised act in relation to this publication may be liable to criminal prosecution and civil claims for damages.

ISBN 9798345625057

For all who love to tell a tale

        and all who love to listen.

Contents

Intro	1
The Prologue to the Glastonbury Tales	
Bro	9
Sandie	15
Suzie	21
Josh	27
Jane	33
Tony	39
Kel	45
Shaznay	51
Sofe	57
Oliver	63
Outro	69
The Glastonbury Tales	
Bro's Tale	77
Sandie's Tale	87
Suzie's Tale	95
Josh's Tale	103
Jane's Tale	111
Tony's Tale	121
Kel's Tale	131
Shaznay's Tale	139
Sofe's Tale	149
Oliver's Tale	157
Close	165
Epilogue	169

Intro

Come gather round and listen well
For there's a tale I'm about to tell
That speaks of folk who are long gone
But whose shadows linger on

Their journeys started all around
From tiny village to built-up town
As they embark upon a quest
To reach the Glastonbury Fest.

From different walks of life they hailed
Ships in the night they usually sailed
But just this once, came one, came all
They united en route to the ball

You'll get to meet each one in turn
And all about them you will learn
Of how they came to join as one
On their way to have some fun

That summer it was set to be
The hottest yet in history
The earth was as dry as Bombay duck
Its dust pretty much to anything stuck

In the ears and up the nose
This summer was simply one of those
Of course, we see them more and more
Since the ice caps started to thaw

The pollen count was off the scale
And everybody prayed for hail
To clear the air and dampen the land
And give Mother Nature a hand

Because back then, that's how it would be
Hot, sunny days and warm evenings you see
None of this squelching around in your wellies
And no comfy coverage at home, on your tellys

A thousand acres set aside
This festival you couldn't hide
The largest for this crammed-in nation
All the others: poor relations

There was only one Glastonbury
Among festivals legendary
People would come from miles around
To join the throbbing, heaving sound

A haze would hover overhead
Filled ecologists with dread…
Visible from space, I'm certain
A fluffy, horizontal curtain

People would burn what they found
The plastic cups all over the ground
To keep their fire burning bright
To dance around all through the night

Of course, now we're all more clued up
Less plastic waste, all bamboo cups
Composting rather than landfill
To help the eco warriors chill

In such an ocean of coloured tents
You'd think that it would make good sense
To attach a trinket of your own
To find your way back home...

But, of course, all who camped here
Were bound to have the same idea...
So, heading for a blue balloon there was always a danger
That you'd end up in the sleeping bag of a total stranger

Still, this was nothing compared with
The leg strength that you had to give
Squatting in a portaloo...
...praying you wouldn't need a poo

Write off washing the whole weekend
'Else it would drive you round the bend
Or try to sneak into VIP
For an actual chair with your cup of tea

The experience of a lifetime
To miss it would have been a crime
Not to want to go was a total mystery
You'd miss a crucial part of history

Brand-new bands and wannabees
Yet sharing centre stage with these
Were guys who'd been around for years
And caused the most almighty cheers

Lazy afternoon poetry recitals
Taking in "am dram" plays was vital
Partying 'til the cows came home
...well, before, 'else where would they roam?

There was so much to see and do
The atmosphere took hold of you
People fat, thin, tall and short
All in its web were caught

So let's embark and meet our stars
Their dreadlocks, glasses, beards and scars
A strange bunch for sure, but we'll soon see
Why they went down in history

The Prologue to the Glastonbury Tales

Bro

Let me begin with a dude named Bro
(Clearly not his real name though)
A hippie left from days gone by
Where sitars twanged and pigs could fly

…but *without* the aid of hallucinogenics
He now drove a bus that was psychedelic
Large enough for a football team
But he really only had one dream

And that was to start up a mobile life
Where he could travel and choose a wife
Well, maybe not just one. Or two…
But take his pick of a fair few

A commune he did hope to start
And all would be loved from the bottom of his heart
Well, maybe a little bit lower than there…
Like, say, in line with his pubic hair

"Make love, not war" was his motto
He was having some trouble though
Finding girls of a similar mind
In these-here safety conscious times

He didn't look bad for his age
With dreaded hair and eyes of sage
Bronzed from wandering 'neath the sun
Chilled days filled with fun

Picking mushrooms, picking fruit
Always in 'lukewarm' pursuit
Of projects tending to the land
And somewhere he could lend a hand

He lived on only nuts and veg
And fruit picked straight from the hedge
Ate nothing with a heartbeat
And wore fake leather on his feet

A vegan life he tried to lead
But sometimes it was hard to heed
Quite often tempted by buttery spread
To cover his crumpets or toasted bread

It was a vice of which he wasn't proud
He never of course would say it aloud
But he enjoyed good food and sharing a feast
If only for the conversation, at least

He was a sociable guy at heart
And always liked to be a part
Meet friends with whom to share a view
...and maybe rudies with a few...

He liked the ladies, that's no lie
And pretty girls always caught his eye
Which sparkled with a youthful wink
And defied his years, you'd think

But girls saw him as a novelty
And when this wore off they were quick to flee
While many liked the romantic notion...
...they soon turned their nose up at his bunion lotion

Years of wearing sandals had taken their effect
His weathered feet were less than perfect
Yes, they certainly allow one's feet to breathe
But one look at those calluses was enough to make you heave

Which wasn't the desired reaction, after all
Here was a man who was constantly on the pull
And despite his feet, rather handsome was he
And eager to give his love away for free

Hippie women who were into all that
He rather digged, being such a cool cat
But many with wrinkles and leathery skin
They weren't always his "thing"

Accompanying him in his bus today
Were two women who'd gone astray
Taken under wing by the size of his heart
Offered shelter and calm and a brand new start

Both his lover, both his friend
Both on him their lives depend
For he had given them hope once more
The will to live and not close the door

They doted on his every word
And didn't think him absurd
Which quite frankly made him happy enough
'cos he knew their lives had been tough

One beaten by a nasty dad
The other, a drunken husband had
But he'd given them a means of escape
"…come on my bus and a nicer road we'll take…"

Sandie

Sandie was slight and quiet as a mouse
But she could eat you right out of house
An insatiable appetite, more and more
You'd think she'd never eaten before

Sandie by name and sandy to the eye
Her mousy hair was brittle and dry
Years of malnutrition had taken their effect
Her skin was prematurely aged, with scarring round her neck

And maybe it was due to this that she now ate and ate
Too many years of no food on her plate
Too many years of a rumbling tum
And waiting for escape to come

Her old man had a problem, of that much she was sure
But unlike other health complaints for this there seemed no cure
One minute he was nice as pie, ever the doting dad
But within the blink of an eye, things would turn so bad

Some days it was fists and others maybe props
He'd use whatever was to hand and pull out all the stops
The belt from round his waist or a pan from the kitchen sink
And it didn't seem to matter whether or not he'd had a drink

There was no rhyme or reason, no flashing warning light
To indicate to Sandie that she should get out of sight
Like a flash of lightening, right out of the blue,
She'd have to dodge a clenched-up fist or duck a flying shoe

There was no humour in her life, nothing to make her smile
Until she happened upon Bro, hung with him for a while
She'd met him in a cafe, in the corner she had hid
Staring at a coffee lake, into her mind she'd slid

A world with no violence, a world she could relax in
A world where life was peaceful and nothing very taxing
Without the constant worry or emotional confusion
She'd escape into her mind and this utopian illusion

"Is this seat taken?" broke into her silent world one day
And little did she know then, happiness had come her way
Bro threw her a smile and snapped her back from space
And with the wink of an eye made the world a better place

Her mouth curled at the corners and broke into a smile
For sikerly, the first this face had seen for a while
As they drank their coffee and started to chat
Sandie's walls were crumbling and that was the start of that...

Now as they packed up Bro's big bus and pulled out through the gate
Excitement filled the air – Sandie couldn't wait
She'd been to Glastonbury before but only as a baby
Her mother's hippie genes had rubbed off on her, maybe

She had faint recollections of lots of smiling faces
And being passed round and round for lots of warm embraces
Memories of happy times – who'd have known to warn her
Of such a cruel hand fate would deal, lurking round the corner

For Sandie's mum was sick you see; not that she'd have said
She always kept her spirits up and wore her happy head
Remaining brave until the end, even having lost her hair
To Sandie, she'd looked just like an angel lying there

So once her mum had passed away, her life turned about-face
The bad moods of her dad became more commonplace
Darkness and emptiness began to take hold
...Sandie had been but 5 years old

Bro had made a blinding start pulling her from the grey
And although her climb still lay ahead, she had come a long way
Sandie now looked forward to what life had in store
And knew she'd be thankful to Bro forevermore

Suzie

Suzie was a rock chick through and through
Evident in everything she'd say and do
She certainly looked the part too
Roadied for Slash and Kiss, to name a few

Leather trousers and leather boots in tow
Always with a rollie on the go
Short front and sides but at the back it flowed
Yes, Suzie wouldn't let that mullet go!

But Suzie had a really doe-eyed face
Which softened her hair's angular embrace
She sauntered along with a certain grace
And above the leather waistband peeked some lace

Hard to put your finger on her years
She'd lived a lot – that much was very clear
Perhaps, you'd guess the big six O was near??
But maybe that was being too severe...

For abuse can take its toll on hair and skin
Sleepless nights and nerves can wear them thin
And deep, dark circles round the eyes begin
And sadness forms a bag below the chin

Suzie had a past, you could just tell
But Bro had brought her right out of her shell
Slowly, she could leave behind the hell
That she had grown to live with all too well

Suzie had been married as a teen
Love-struck by the not-so-American dream
Bumped into him while listening to Cream
He was the hottest thing she'd ever seen

A jaw line to be envied by most guys
Piercing, dark and moody russet eyes
Big, strong arms and tight leather-clad thighs
His power should have come as no surprise

Their love affair was wonderful to start
Passionate and soulful from the heart
So when the fruit eventually turned tart
Suzie found it very hard to part

They enjoyed a social life to admire
Among their friends, their humour wouldn't tire
Recounting yarns together, they were on fire
As the alcohol consumed grew higher and higher

They'd often bicker once they'd had a drink
Standard for some couples, you may think
But Suzie tried to catch it at the brink
No choice but to be the one to shrink

They were both dependent, before they knew
Suzie realised first, this wouldn't do
Her only cure for the morning-after blues
Was to crack open another bottle… or two

So Suzie quit - enough was enough
Alcohol no more. Though it was tough
She knew the road ahead would get rough
As each day her husband grew more gruff

He sure had a temper, that's no lie
Rash words and off the handle he would fly
Like a time bomb she could feel the days tick by
Knowing soon it would be time again to cry

Never knowing how each day would turn out
Never knowing what was going to make him shout
Not always sure what each row was about
But pretty sure she'd end up with a clout

He'd turn up at home so late at night
And straight away the tension was tight
Deep down Suzie knew she should take flight
As this could only end up in a fight

He'd be unkempt and have red on his cheeks
Of cheap perfume and whisky he would reek
He cheated on her every other week
And Suzie knew her future looked bleak

Yet somehow she found it hard to leave
A web of lovely memories she'd weave
Sometimes she would find it hard to breathe
Remembering how their hearts were on their sleeves

But who could tell where things had fallen apart
Should Suzie have seen this right from the start?
It's easy to ignore your head and listen to your heart
And let things ferment rather than upset the apple cart

It was a bright and sunny day when Bro had come to town
He spotted Suzie in Central Park, lost behind her frown
Tried to lift her thoughts, though her spirits were down
And sure enough the grass turned green, from its muddy brown

An escape to England sure had its pull
No longer would she feel like a fool
Living with a man now so cruel
When this guy here was nothing but cool

She made the move and boarded the plane
Threw her marriage down the nearest drain
Left behind the torment and the pain
Never to see her drunken spouse again

Josh

Josh was a ladies' man, this much will unfurl
At every swanky venue on both arms a different girl
Tanned straight from the bottle, or maybe a sunbed
The best groomed hair you've ever seen sat upon his head

He'd wear the latest fashions, but only if smooth
Nothing chav or tacky – he had nothing to prove
He could afford the best so the best is what he bought
Wore everything with style – a skill that can't be taught

He'd often fly to Paris, New York or Milan
Private jet of course, as only the wealthy can
He liked to keep a finger on the pulse of the world
And keep, in every town, a finger on a different girl

He certainly was popular among the fairer sex
They liked his swanky clothes and the muscles that he flexed
They liked the lavish gifts that he'd buy them night and day
And hoped that maybe one day he would stay

But they could be waiting for some time
Settling down to him seemed like a crime
Why would he stick with just one girl who was hot
When he could have his pick of the lot

He liked to play the wide-boy, he liked to flash his cash
He liked to throw huge parties and get completely smashed
Invariably the fuzz would show to break up all the fun
But they'd be swayed to turn a cheek, when all was said and done

He earned so much that some folk often gave a frown
But nothing changed because he pretty much owned the whole town
Still, he did give something back, the booze and coke ran free
And no doubt the odd STI and unwanted pregnancy…

He wanted to experience the festival scene
He'd heard the girls were easy 'cos they're all on speed
He thought he'd sign some new acts and maybe book a band
To play at his next party, the biggest bash he'd ever planned

And so he joined the motley crew to add to the load
His Maserati burnt out at the side of the road
His breakdown cover arranged by his P.A. who clearly shirked
And who'd be straight out the door when he got back to work

Usually a simple call he would have made
But there'd be no taxi cab rushing to his aide
The signal here was terrible, he'd have to have a word
As he couldn't have poor coverage stopping him being heard

How hard could it be anyway, to set up an ISP
He'd put it to his board, to expand the company
Another finger, another pie to make some more money
And more staff to employ of course… female, preferably

That said, Josh tended to avoid kicking up a stink
By dipping his pen in the company ink
He liked to give the press and public something on which to think
So to an unknown beauty he'd much rather be linked

Across tabloid covers his face was often smeared
Next to a gorgeous babe it usually appeared
Leaving a nightclub avoiding the hordes
Or on the red carpet at some music awards

And sometimes with a new signed act
What he was famous for, in fact
It's what started him on his road to riches
An eye for talent and a talent for pitches

When Josh was only 18 he had managed a mate's band
And the journey he'd mapped out for them went exactly as planned
He had the gift of the gab and luck thrown in to boot
And soon he'd got them seen by all the influential suits

From strength to strength they soared, a whirlwind success
And Josh's pot was filling up, as you may well guess
Yes his bank account was bulging, he was loving the fame
And his trousers bulged too, his lust knowing no shame

With girls swarming round him, like wasps drawn to a bun
Josh would sample all on offer, he was having so much fun
They loved him for his money, they loved him for the press
And it didn't hurt he didn't need to dress to impress...

With a clatter and a clunk, this bright bus pulled into view
So, taking up Bro's offer, he joined this motley crew
Still, a lift was a lift and you never really knew
Who would prove to maybe be of use to you...

Jane

Plain Jane she was known as to all her family
Always stuck with her head in a book on anthropology
She didn't care for fashion or all the latest trends
She didn't care for anyone because she had no friends

Her family, well, they really did despair
Wished she'd do something with her awful hair
Told her they wished she'd change her look
Which just drove her deeper into a book

She looked much older than her years
With hair scragged back behind her ears
And clothes less Tatler, more just tat
That even your gran would turn her nose up at

Her glasses, broken through neglect, were fixed with a sticky plaster
Well, why waste money on a new pair, only to end once again in disaster
Her skin though, was immaculate – it never saw the sun
'Cos suffering from sunburn wasn't her idea of fun

She was a model student, always attended class
Kept her eye on everyone through 4mm glass
It was easy to forget when masked by those frames
That she wasn't looking in on some 3D, VR game

She viewed them all as subjects: mice in her maze
Blending into the background she could follow them round for days
Interesting what people do, without deliberation
When blissfully unaware that they are under observation

She liked to study people; see what made them tick
How they dealt with lows and how they got their kicks
Of course, she'd never partake herself, but she knew all of the ways
To spend high nights and hallucinogenic days

She knew one of the "techy" lads, who volunteered in the science labs
She'd managed to buy chemicals, from fizzy pills to acid tabs
On occasion she would "slip" and into someone's drink they'd land
It wasn't mean… purely for research, you understand

The results could be quite different, from the manic to the still
And occasionally if the coast was clear, she'd ask them how they feel
Some had been informative and she had learnt much from it
Less so from a lad whose stomach was bad and she'd ended up covered in vomit

Sometimes, purely for the cause, she'd telephone her peers
Pretend that they had been expelled and monitor their tears
Under a staff name she had anonymity
And could meddle with emotions, then just walk away, scot-free

After their ordeal, Jane would watch them from afar
See if they hit the books or chose to hit the bar
If the first, she'd join them and try to get them talking
The latter she'd offer a ride, as they often had trouble walking

Hazardous, it could be, getting them to share
Reveal how they were feeling – if indeed they cared
The sober could be wary as to why she held a pen
And with the drunks there was always the risk she'd be covered in vomit again…

The festival scene would be a treat to behold
Tonnes of clueless lab rats, so she'd been told
She could be invisible within the swarming masses
And keep a noteful eye on all the other lads and lasses

Her parents thought her naive and weren't overjoyed
She raised an eyebrow and tried not to get annoyed
She decided it was so much easier to pretend
So she made it clear she wasn't heading off without a friend

"*...but Tony's going mum and I'll be with all his mates*"
Her brother was streetwise, so they avoided a debate
"*I promise that I won't wander off all on my own*"
They put their trust in the maturity he'd shown

Little did they know, from that, her intentions were far
She'd paid Tony off with chores and offered to fill his car
Lied that she'd okayed it first with Mum and Dad
But she planned to lose Tony the first chance that she had

He, of course, would not care less whether she stuck around
Though they were close, his friends thought her a little odd, she'd found
He knew that she was sensible and wouldn't get into strife
So he'd allowed her to tag along, for an easy life

Tony

Jane's brother Tony couldn't be less like her
Surrounded by friends - he was Mister Popular
Blessed with brains and blessed with looks
Certainly buried his head in different books

At Maths and Science he did excel
But generally did very well
At any subject they could find
To occupy his open mind

His deep blue eyes were large as lakes
His lips as plump as fairy cakes
His looks could have led him to modelling
But that really wasn't him

His hair was thick and fairly floppy
...made the girls all go quite soppy
They thought him cute with his cheeky smile
And tried to hang around a while

But Tony had no time to spare
For girls at the moment, he didn't much care
To a greater cause he'd have to yield
Centred around the playing field

He liked to play. He liked to win
Hockey and Rugby were his thing
His muscles were toned, but in an athletic manner
So he didn't fling his t-shirt off and go all Bruce Banner

He didn't work out in the gym – preferred to train with friends
Truly a team player through and through to the end
Whenever he improved, it would benefit them all
And not just put a trophy on his wall

But Tony had a secret that he kept to himself
Hidden at the back of a wardrobe shelf
Tiny orcs and goblins in a world quite fantastic
Painted intricately and made of plastic

He'd like to game, and be "that guy"
But so far had remained quite shy
With his mates: had to keep face
Didn't want there to be a trace

Wouldn't do to be caught on the hop
Sneaking off into Games Workshop
'Do nothing at all for his street cred.
On a stick they'd have his head

And so he'd stay behind closed doors
With battles raging on the floor
He'd paint his troops under lamp light
A halogen beam in the dark of night

He'd always been a street-smart kid, a good head on his shoulders
He looked wise behind his eyes, you'd think he was much older
Martial Arts since he was 6 had built on discipline
And hadn't hurt either with any trouble he'd landed in

Not that he was angst – he was very level headed
And quite honestly, those were the moments that he dreaded
A mate gets in a fight; gets ideas above his station
So Tony would always step in to diffuse the situation

Tony knew that fighting wasn't the way to go
But being such a babe magnet, things sometimes came to blows
In a nightclub, who's to know if a pretty girl is single?
Until her fella appears and threatens to flatten you like a Pringle

But Tony often managed to talk his way out
Avoid using his fists to give the other guy a clout
It didn't always work of course, but sometimes they were charmed
…or perhaps the strength of his handshake, left them alarmed

He was the golden child – to his folks, could do no wrong
So knowing he was going, allowed Jane to tag along
They knew that he would keep her safe; his friends too – keep an eye
On their oddball Jane – so different – and so painfully shy

They set off early in the morning, laden with goodies
Plans made already to hook up with his hoodies
Beers, Pot Noodles, Rizlas and a bag of a certain "stuff"
Which he hid from Jane, knowing she thought better of her bruv

It wasn't long before the engine made an awful noise
And knowing nothing about cars, not one of those boys
With his head under the bonnet, parts swimming before his eyes
Out of nowhere he heard a lazy *"need some help, you guys?"*

And so, when Bro was unable to get the engine started
As he was heading the same way, no point in being parted
With room on the bus to take all of their things
They hopped on board and so grew larger, this gathering

Kel

Kel was known through bryn and vale
As über-chav and epic fail
His hair was spiked, not that you'd know
For he wore a cap wherever he would go

Lots of chains. Lots of bling
Never paid more than a score for anything
Different suit for every day...
...tracksuit that is, ideal for work and play

He'd do a bit of that. He'd do a bit of this
Worked part-time in Burger King and then go on the piss
He liked to start trouble, fighting was his game
He clearly had a complex from having a girl's name

It didn't help that he wasn't the tallest fellow
Wouldn't do, of course, to be seen to be yellow
Every Friday night was just as bad
Piss up, then a bust up, then off home with a kebab

He'd find the smallest thing about which to pick a fight
It never took much, being such a gobshite
His Welsh accent was strong, sometimes all it took
Was a snigger or a whisper or even a fleeting look

You could say he was paranoid or even sensitive
But in fact he simply liked to fight – it's how he chose to live
You'd think his mates would tire, but in fact they would entice
Spur him on, give verbal, then scurry away like mice

They constantly were round his gaff, all having part-time jobs
They pinched whatever they thought could be worth a few bob
Devoured what food they could find, as they were all skint
Always outstayed their welcome, never taking the hint

It mostly washed over Kel – he was so out of touch
They took advantage of him wanting to be liked so much
He didn't always get he was the brunt of the joke
He'd laugh along with them as they all sat there and smoked

One time they'd popped him loads of pills, but he had been quite clueless
And he'd ended up stripping off and ran to the hills, shoeless
Kel too, of course, could dish it out and not be backed into the wall
...but spare a thought for his poor mum, 'cos he still lived at home, after all...

He may be gobby with his mates, but his mum was really the boss
"Yes – you can stay out late, but God help you if you don't floss!"
With his dad gone his mum dragged him up by the ears
His only role model, she had ruled the roost for years

He tried to keep the truth from her, not liking him to fight
But she knew exactly what occurred, and how he spent his nights
Kel joined the bus with a thumb in the air and a board, on the motorway
His mates had arranged their own way there and not given him a say

"*Let's all meet at the gates*" they'd said, and Kel had nodded along
Packed up his bag and off he'd headed: nothing could go wrong
No-one stopped for hours and hours – lucky it wasn't colder
And then this bus, all covered in flowers, pulled up on the hard shoulder...

Shaznay

Hopping on with Kelly was his girlfriend of two years
The biggest hoops you've ever seen hanging from her ears
Nails so long she'd be hard pushed to open a can of drink
And her hair pulled back so tight, it's surprising she could blink

She'd managed to persuade her mum to babysit Bianca
Didn't stop, of course, for a second though to thank her
Grabbed a tiny bag and out the door she'd run
Off to meet her Kelly and off to have some fun

Their baby Bianca was one year old
It definitely was Kel's. …or so he'd been told
Shaznay's past was colourful, so it was quite hard to know
But she did have his spiky hair and a Burberry babygrow

Shaznay had been around the block, some called her the local bike
Curious from an early age, she'd wondered what it was like
Boredom maybe? Rebellion? Lust perhaps – who knew?
Over a short space of time her reputation grew

Just a bit of fun – didn't mean a thing
She was up for it all after a bottle of White Lightening
Not very fussy, so long as they were kind
And didn't want to do weird stuff, she really didn't mind

One time she'd met with Evan as soon as school was out
And they'd done it up against a tree when no-one was about
Another day, with Rhys, at break, in a secluded spot
But they'd been caught by Miss Davies and detention they had got

At a party one weekend she'd met a lad who'd taught
How to have a fumble and not get your zipper caught
Whenever chance arose, she'd have a good try
But eventually, of course, her luck would run dry

Too young to be confined by fleeting infatuations
Too young to take seriously the knock-on implications
Too young to understand what the fuss was all about
But not too young to partake and regularly put out

But then she had met Kel and something had changed
Primarily her belly, and their lives were rearranged
Who knows if they had not found out that they were expecting
If she would have stayed with him, or moved on to the next thing

They'd decided not to wed and they still lived apart
But Kel had been there for them both, right from the start
Their mums agreed there wasn't enough cash to go around
So there'd be no flat, no wedding and no real solution found

Most likely it was for the best and saved on aggravation
And, after all, Shaznay still aimed to finish her education
...for she was 17 and now 9 months behind
Having a baby during GCSEs has that effect, you'll find

She certainly was a sight to behold
Teamed her tracksuit with *lots* of gold
Fake designer bag from the back of a van
To match her fake hair colour... laugh... and tan

Sunkissed wasn't exactly the look that she'd achieved
More "you've been Tangoed" than MTV
She wanted to be Kim K, Jade T or Cheryl Cole
But sadly closer to David Dickinson, on the whole

Her friends were all as orange, teamed with white tracksuits
Although hardly appropriate for outdoor pursuits
Her hoodie didn't fit well, with its zip made of plastic
...and her stomach rested slightly on the top of the elastic

They were very close, all from the same town
Loved a bit of shopping and a night out at The Crown
Drank too much and would end up in a fight
A lairy end to their lairy night

Determined not to lose out on the fun that could be missed
Made arrangements with the other girls to get completely pissed
"*Meet at the festival*" had sounded good
So she resigned herself to get there any way she could

And so...
With her bestie and fella in tow...
The bus it did a-trundle, left ways and right
The bus picked up these three and trundled right out of sight…

Sofe

Shaznay's best mate Sofe was always on the shark
She'd snogged boys almost everywhere – the bus stop and the park
She had a pretty face and a tiny little frame
And the boys would hover round her, 'cos they all thought she was game

Dark, bouncy hair that hung down her back
But pulled into a ponytail to fit in with the pack
A small and rounded chest she had developed now
But pushed up with a Wonderbra for maximum ker-pow

Her eyes were meadow green, much lighter than the norm
It seemed the sun would shine from them when she was on top form
And sometimes they'd look grey, like a cloud was overhead
And at those times, that shining light was dead…

Shaznay loved her like a sis. She thought that it was sad
That Sofe didn't have a mum, but lived with her nan and dad
She didn't know, of course, that our Sofe was well-to-do
And certainly used to have a bob or two

For her real name was Sophia and Papa would be appalled
If he knew each time she left the house that he was being fooled
Her skirt became a dress - an immediate transformation
The band hugged her chest, not leaving much to the imagination

Fluent in French and German, to boot
She really was clever as well as a beaut
Played the piano like Mylene Klass
Yet insisted on living this farce

Her mother was from the money you see
But Sophia's life had not turned out quite how it should be
Mother decided a carefree life in France she would prefer
And having a child at such a young age simply wasn't her

So thanks to an AWOL mum and AWOL money too
Sophia and her dad had to give up all that they knew
His wages were enough to put dinner on the plate
But they moved in with her nan in a block on the estate

She kept it all inside – not to be talked about
Questions and judging she could quite do without
Her mum, her past, her present, left her filled with doubt
And dwelling on deep feelings made her heart and brain shout

Why had Mother left them – was it all her fault?
Had she driven her away? She'd puzzle at the thought
Sophia had been six when her world went down the drain
She'd thought she'd been a happy child - never been a pain

Never answered back; never caused a scene
Never said spiteful things, she hated being mean
She had nothing to moan about, her life had been serene
So why had Mother run away and shattered the dream

Her dad had been amazing – her hero and her friend
But her brain was too broken for even him to mend
She really loved him dearly, but would never let him see
How messed up she was inside: this other person she would be

She loved all the attention, loved meeting new boys
With a few on the go at any time, they acted as white noise
Drowned out all her doubts; drowned out all her fears
And filled this gaping emptiness that had grown over the years

Putting on a front made her bold, made her tough
Even if she often seemed to others a bit rough
It meant she sat quite cozy with the girls on the estate
And Shaznay took her underwing and now was her best mate

She joined them for the festival – what a fun distraction
Never wanting to be one to miss out on the action
Pop a few pills and pop her festival cherry
So, this bus picked up Sofe – Kel and Shaznay's gooseberry…

Oliver

Oliver was pretty smart and pretty funny too
Anyone who was anyone he pretty much knew
He was pretty fashionable and his voice a pretty sound
In fact, Oliver was just plain pretty all round

He had his own style, liked to twist with his own flair
He wore the faintest eyeliner and small beads in his hair
A matted mess of hairspray, yet sculpted with great care
Certainly his appearance caused many an eye to stare

For Oliver was chiselled, a face without a flaw
He had a nose and cheekbones many women would kill for
But his chin was broad and strong, masculine to the core
In fact, everyone's head would turn when he walked through the door

He was quite theatrical but not too OTT
He wore his heart on his sleeve for everyone to see
Refreshingly honest, it just came naturally
And he really did believe this was the only way to be

He wore mostly black, but always with a flash
Of electric blue or parrot green, just to make a splash
He wore a mix of styles but somehow they didn't clash
Not so much "on trend", but oozing with his own panache

When he spun a yarn he'd bring a smile to your face
Transform into an audience anyone within his space
Quick witted, many found it hard to keep the pace
And some would get offended when he put them in their place

He liked to entertain, liked to raise a laugh
Often at others' expense, who dared to cross his path
He'd cut them down with ease, shrinking them by half
But pick them right back up after, as was his autograph

"Friends" were few and far between, although he was well known
Oliver seemed to spend a lot of time all on his own
Of course, he was at every party that was ever thrown
And being such a handsome lad, he never left alone

But the girls that would depart with him weren't always that much cop
Sure, they were hot enough to make traffic stop
And sure, they had the bodies to make your jaw drop
But, the problem was, they didn't always have that much up-top

Oliver so longed for mental stimulation
Not present in most girls showering him with adulation
He knew she must exist somewhere across the nation
Someone upon which he could pour infatuation

To really make him think – give him ideas on which to dwell
To really make him laugh – someone out of her shell
To really make him open up, though she would never tell
And to really make him horny wouldn't hurt, as well

Yes, Oliver had an insatiable appetite
For devouring young ladies all through the night
He was so debonair, they'd not put up a fight
But some were quite relieved when the end was in sight

Most would depart, certainly by morning
Kicked out of his flat while they were still yawning
And quite often without any fair warning
They'd find they'd leave behind some of the clothes they'd been adorning

None held his attention enough to keep around
All would bore him terribly by daybreak, he found
He wanted to find someone who shared a common ground
Then he'd throw himself in for a penny, in for a pound

He'd been to Glastonbury many times before
He liked to hitch a lift, the train was such a chore
All the tickets and the timetables and chewing gum on the floor
He found a ride with new-found friends suited him much more

And who could tell, just who he might meet along the way
Someone who could hold his interest for the whole day?
Someone who he'd actually care what they had to say?
So out he stuck his thumb and prepared himself to play…

Outro

So as this jaunt got off the ground
A pastime needed to be found
To fill with words their travelling day
And make the minutes tick away

The journey many hours would take
This bus would rattle, judder and shake
If pushed too hard to build up pace
As after all, it wasn't a race

Some were, of course, known to each other
The odd boyfriend, sister or brother
But Oliver thought it would be fun
To learn something about everyone

As he was on his tod, you see
A long drive it would surely be
With no one else to have a natter
To sit alone while others chattered

And so he spoke, to see who's in
If others fancied joining him
"A little game, to pass the time
And maybe earn yourself a dime??"

Probably more from awkwardness
They all gave a resounding *"yes"*
So that was that; the gavel fell
And now they each a tale would tell

A story drawn from their own life
That spoke of fun or love or strife
And at the end, when all had spoken
The winner would receive a token

All would chip in to a pot
It didn't have to be a lot
For there were ten to make it up
And put into the collection cup

And this money, it could be spent
However the winner's fancy went
Be it drugs or booze or clothes
Or even vegeburgers, if they chose

Clearly it was just incentive
To tell a tale the most inventive
To keep the others wanting more
And try their hardest not to bore

Factually based it was supposed to be
Though none would know, in all honesty
If truth were bent or a little swollen
So long as the crowd's attention was stolen

To judge only on mirth would not be wise
Nor if the tale brought tears to the eyes
Nor if adventure so extreme
You felt as though it were a dream

For "spooky" could be one man's vice
But for another, not so nice
So each would score from one to ten
For how each tale had pleasured them

That clearly was the fairest way
Then everybody would have their say
The scores would be put anonymously
Into the pot, so none could see

Until they all had said their piece
And the journey had near ceased
Then the numbers could be seen
And they could crown their king or queen

So off we go – let's get stuck in
Settle down as the tales begin
Relax, breathe deep, open your mind
And let's see where this road will wind…

The Glastonbury Tales

Bro's Tale

Back when I was just a boy
I always had a favourite toy
Everywhere with me he'd come
I loved him more than anyone

Rosy cheeks and jet-black hair
A bow tie round his neck he'd wear
Pinstriped suit, spats as well
A wooden jaw which rose and fell…

A dummy see – you get my gist
Belonged once to a ventriloquist
But cast away, as if rotten
And left in the dark, to be forgotten

Many years I guess passed by
His paint flaked off, his joints grew dry
Damp and dust had taken toll
On this here old ventriloquist doll

Then one day he had found himself
Sat up high on a junk shop shelf
Out of sightline for most passers-by
But not for a child with a wandering eye

"*Mummy, mummy!*" I'd said with elation
Whilst tugging the hem of her latest creation
I pointed up high with a big, wide grin
"*Please, please, PLEASE can I have him?!*"

So, home we went, my new toy in tow
And pretty soon he stole the show
Because my other toys just weren't the same
Their eyes in one position, would remain…

But Tarquin's eyes moved left to right
The first time it happened gave me quite a fright
I guess they had been stuck before
Jammed up with dust from the shelf in the store

I don't know how Tarquin became his name
I just said it one day whilst playing a game
I don't remember hearing it on TV
It just, sort of, well, fell out of me

One night whilst laying in my bed
It kept going round and round in my head
What to call my new-found chum?
"Tarquin" popped to the tip of my tongue

I must have heard it surely, but it seemed
As though it came to me in a dream
There weren't any "Tarquins" at my school
Still, I thought it sounded pretty cool

We'd play for hours, us two boys
He was much more real than my other toys
I could make him talk and his eyes, now freed
Quite often seemed to follow me…

One day I was looking through the windowpane
It was dark outside and starting to rain
I thought I saw, in the faint reflection
His eyes looking straight in my direction

I spun round quickly, my heart filled with dread
But of course, they were staring straight ahead
A trick of the light, or my brain running wild
The silly thoughts of an imaginative child

I studied well at that young age
Eager to learn and turn each page
School was enjoyable, I had good fun
But I always loved going home to Mum

One afternoon she was waiting outside
A look on her face that she couldn't hide
Anger? Hurt? Disappointment?
One hand on her hip – very poignant

"How could you?" she said, *"We're not made of money
And wipe that grin off, this isn't funny"*
So shocked was I, it took me a while
To sense her mood and drop my smile

"What do you mean? I don't understand?"
She shook her head and grabbed my hand
Marched me through into my room
And thrust at me the kitchen broom

What lay before me was a mess
And news to me, I must confess
My teddies ripped, fluff sticking out
Eyes and ears strewn all about

My soldiers melted in a puddle
My cars and trucks all in a muddle
Wheels stripped off, all in bits
And to think Mum thought I'd done all this!

I was confused and I was shaken
I must tell mum she was mistaken
But then a thought crept through my head
What to tell her had happened *instead?*...

Very slowly I turned my head
And there sat at the foot of my bed
Tarquin with a vacant stare
I didn't remember leaving him there…

As if to laugh, his jaw hung low
Now I was being silly though
What a thought; what a notion!
A toy causing such commotion!

Tarquin *was* just that you see
An old ventriloquist dummy
Nothing more. How could he be?
Even if he sometimes felt real to me

Later that same very year
Something happened that was most queer
Left me questioning my brain
And whether, in fact, I'd gone insane!

We had a Science Fayre at school
Held in the main assembly hall
Projects worked on for weeks and weeks
On the big day, final tweaks

A few of us needed a hand
To bring them through to the main stand
So to my classroom, off I shot
To meet up with the other lot

First to arrive; ran through the door
But couldn't believe what I saw
I covered my mouth to stifle a cry
As mayhem lay before my eyes

Jim's project was covered in glue
You couldn't now tell what it was supposed to do
White gunk dripped through all its parts
It pained me to my very heart

My project smashed, parts thrown about
It made me want to scream and shout
Two months I'd spent, adjusting here and there
Getting it ready for the Science Fayre

But worst of all, right at the back
Ruth's project had been attacked
It was the cleverest of all
But now it wasn't standing tall

Engulfed in flames it sagged and popped
With smoke bellowing from the top
You couldn't tell what it was before
And no one now would be in awe

And then I got the biggest scare
For propped up in my classroom chair
With open jaw and eyes so wide
Arms hung loosely by his side…

Tarquin – but how could this be?
Tarquin? I hadn't brought him with me!
Tarquin? I must be going crazy…
TARQUIN??! But he's just an old dummy?!!!

I picked him up and ran away
I knew what everyone would say
I'd get the blame – it would be my fault
If either of us there were caught

I kept on running, I knew not where
I didn't look back – I didn't dare
So much anger, and so, so sad
I'd never, ever felt this bad

All my friends… What would they think?!
The thought of them made my heart sink
As heavy as my heart was my rucksack
But I ran and I ran and I never went back

Sandie's Tale

Trifle was my favourite dessert as a girl
The very thought of trifle would make my toes curl
It didn't really matter much about the exact flavour
I just couldn't wait for the different tastes to savour

The scrumptious, creamy topping with chocolate flakes scattered
The thick custard layer next, was what mattered
But then, the fruity base, all surrounded by jelly
And spongey lady finger cakes resting on its belly

I could eat a whole bowl if it were allowed
But generally my mum only made one for a crowd
If friends were round, or family, so it wasn't ever fitting
For me to get stuck in and devour the whole thing

It's my earliest memory, of taking my small bowl
The plastic kind, with a plastic spoon, and eating my piece whole!
For I was only little, so a little I was served
I really wanted more, but I didn't have the nerve

I sat on my cushion looking at my empty dish
For it to be full again, was what I wished
The adults' spoons waved around, as their lips bleated
While I was left, empty-bowled, feeling rather cheated

Some grown-ups were wasteful, they'd leave some on their plates
And not even offer it round to their mates
Pushed aside, discarded, while they chatted on with mirth
Rudely unaware it was the greatest dish on earth!

I guess I should have made a noise, if only they had known
It could have been passed to me and not simply thrown
But maybe not, as often I had seen Mum roll her eyes
"*You'll get fat*!" she'd scoff, at anyone questioning her portion size

Mum was very willowy, she walked as though on air
She wore handmade clothes and beads in her hair
Not one for excess, she was very restrained
She'd never overeat, so slender she remained

Looking back, I wonder now, was something else at play
Quite often we wouldn't eat a thing for the whole day
Mum and Dad sometimes seemed high, dancing round the house
Then, at other times, they'd both be quiet as a mouse

I would get so hungry, too small to reach the shelves
Into any lower cupboards I would try to delve
But not much to be found, nothing to be had
And I certainly didn't want to get caught out by Dad

When Mum was there Dad always seemed fairly laid back
But as soon as she wasn't, he was quick to attack
"Stupid child! Get your hands out where I can see them!"
"Stop doing this!" "Stop doing that!" …time and time again

Mum was more obliging, if she could only concentrate
She'd always get distracted, so, no food upon my plate
Mum made the greatest trifle – for that she set the bar
But I really can't recall anything else in her repertoire…

I remember beans on toast. I remember bread and jam
I remember wishing there were more beans in that can…
I remember being hungry almost every single night
But I knew that I was loved when my mum held me tight

One weekend, one summer, the whole town was filled with glee
A royal celebration – there was to be a big party
Our street was to be closed, with chairs and tables lined
And everyone was bringing food or drink of some kind

My mum, of course, would contribute a trifle for the day
But not just any trifle – that wouldn't do, no way!
This was to be the greatest trifle Mum had ever made
A trifle so fantastic it put all others in the shade

The bowl was so enormous I could probably bathe in it
When finished, for a king and queen it certainly was fit
Lavishly decorated: chocolate, fruit and piped cream
It really was the grandest trifle I had ever seen

On a table it was put, while all celebrated
The thought of others tucking in got me agitated
With one eye on the trifle I pretended things were fine
But I wondered if there was a way that trifle could be mine

I knew that it was greedy and with others I should share
But I just loved trifle so, SO much I really didn't care!
I knew that I would get told off, if I were to get spotted
But I carried on regardless and my sneaky plan I plotted…

With all eyes on the big screen, I slipped off from the crowd
Nobody noticed, as the atmosphere was loud
I ran into our garden, fetched a bucket and a spade
And set about making the biggest pie I'd ever made

It didn't take me long, there was lots lying around
And I mixed up just about everything that I found
Mud, grass, worms and a beetle or two
Some pebbles and some leaves and the lace from an old shoe

I topped it all off with some flowers from a pot
Then wrapped a length of garden wire round the whole lot
No, it wasn't trifle and it wasn't topped with cream
But I was proud: it was a mud pie fit for a queen!

I picked the bucket up, toppling on my tiny feet
I reached the corner of our house and crept out to the street
The coast was clear: I made a dash and stretched myself up high
And swapped that lovely trifle for my glorious mud pie

Feeling very clever I ran home to our shed
And for what seemed like hours, on that trifle I fed
It tasted just as wonderful as it had appeared
I enjoyed every mouthful, while the inevitable neared

I can still remember those strawberries – so sweet!
And that custard and that chocolate – it was SO good to eat
I can still remember the smoothness of that cream
…and I can still remember the sound of Mum's scream

It didn't take long, of course, for me to get caught
For I was very young and not as clever as I thought
The culprit would be found; daft to think that I could duck it
For all would know that it was me: dad recognised his bucket

Mum was fine and once the shock wore off, she didn't care
Neighbours whispered, shook their heads and gathered round to stare
Some found it amusing but sensed there was trouble looming
As all the while, Dad looked on, absolutely fuming

I hadn't meant it nastily or to cause any upset
I'd simply wanted trifle and MORE than I'd always get!
It taught me early lessons about greed …and about Dad
And the look that flushed behind his eyes whenever he was mad

And things were to get much, much worse once Mum sadly departed
Dad always seemed angry as well as broken-hearted
Little did I know then what my life was to become
But I still adore trifle and I still adore my mum

Suzie's Tale

I would lay on my back, for hours on my bed
Miles away from where I lay, hands behind my head
I'd stare at him, this gorgeous guy, at that hair and those eyes
It's amazing, when daydreaming, just how fast time flies

Steve Tyler covered every inch of my wall space
Everywhere I looked, staring back, his lovely face
To say I was besotted wasn't an exaggeration
Call it what you will – a teenage infatuation

Not quite when I was old enough, I got my first tattoo
Hurt like hell but felt so cool, as it was so taboo
I really felt the business when I sauntered down the street
And I'd look over my shades at anyone who I would meet

I learned to play guitar, but I never would be great
My head in the clouds, I found it hard to concentrate
The learning took so long – I just couldn't be fagged!
No matter how much my music teacher nagged

I preferred to listen and to rock out to a band
Or mosh around my room, the music loud as I could stand
I went to gigs whenever I had dollars to my name
I loved being surrounded by the buzz and sniff of fame

Drunken nights out at The Rat were a weekly affair
Such a high, working all day, then we'd all meet up there
My friends and I were local and we knew all of the staff
And no matter what the band were like we'd always have a laugh

Some would go on to be big and some would fade away
Even those who had fizzled out were no doubt glad to play
The Rat was so iconic you could often spot a star
While heading to the washrooms or hanging at the bar

I would start the night out with a wild anticipation
Not knowing what's to come, but without hesitation
I was always up for it: The beer. The flirt. The game
But inevitably outcomes were generally the same

I'd wake up in the morning with a head like Bonzo's drum
Mouth as furry as a dog, teeth fuzz-coated by rum
My neck and ears were aching and my hair would stink of smoke
And, oh Jeez, what on earth had I seen in that bloke?!...

Beer goggles certainly had much to answer for
Never my intention when I headed out the door
A guy who seemed a hottie when he stopped and looked my way
Often was less of a catch in the cold light of day

The exception to this rule was when Tommy came along
There we were, both rocking out full whack to a great song
His long hair thrashing back and forth was thrilling to watch
And sent a lightning bolt straight to my crotch

The sexiest guy I had ever seen in person
His butt in those leather pants – my self-restraint worsened
His biceps bulging nicely from his white sleeveless tee
His eyes were dark and smouldering – just like hot coffee

We got on like a house on fire – really hit it off
A true whirlwind – moved so fast even my friends had scoffed
He became my world and he was all that I could see
A shame I didn't take the time to keep an eye on me

I guess I had been naive to believe I was enough
I was so young and really thought we were so in love
I should have seen the signs, they had been there all along
And I knew down in my stomach how he treated me was wrong

Another drink. Another girl. Just another night.
Another drink. Another girl. Just another fight.
I would make excuses for him, turn the other cheek
But life continued to taste bitter week after week

Each time he was mean I lost a little part of me
Stripped back to my branches; all the leaves gone from my tree
Vulnerable and lonely, I stuck around like glue
Not always easy doing what you know you should do

Perhaps a part of me wished that he would make the break
He clearly didn't want me – our real love had turned to fake
That must have spurred me on to do the crazy thing I did
Hoping he would storm out and I'd finally be rid...

While tackling the horror that is the aisles of Walmart
Avoiding mums and prams, shielded safely by my cart
I found myself pondering which shampoo to buy
When in my head a light came on, as something caught my eye

Seemed strange to me that they should be positioned side by side
One to show it off, while the other to try to hide
How awful it would be if they were to get confused
And instead of nice shampoo, a hair removal cream was used

I laughed out loud, then stopped myself to think the idea through
Would it really be such a terrible thing to do?
I thought of all the pain this man had made me endure
And I grabbed that bottle, paid the price, I'd never been more sure

At home I sat nervously nibbling at my nails
What had I done and would I even live to tell the tale
There was no way in hell that Tommy ever could find out
This had to be an accident, or he'd do more than shout

I submerged in hot water that bottle of Neet
(What a pointless exercise re-branding it as Veet?!)
I scraped off all the printing so all that remained
Was the word "hair" here and there, and nothing of its name

I emptied half the contents so that it would seem old
Women keep this stuff for ages, or so I'm told
Tommy took such little notice of me those days
That he wouldn't have a clue about my bathroom ways

I placed the bottle on the rack, positioned it well
Exactly where the shampoo lived, next to the shower gel
It wouldn't be my fault – it would simply be bad luck
If he accidentally happened to pick that bottle up

The evening came and yet again an argument arose
What was it about that time? Heaven only knows...
It was obvious that Tommy planned a night out on the drink
And to hook up with one of his other women, I should think

At least that relinquished any feelings of guilt
When the proverbial milk was inevitably spilt
An hour, maybe, had passed as he'd gone upstairs to preen
And then it came; a loud, almost blood-curdling scream

I couldn't resist witnessing this for myself
But I did it from a distance for the sake of my health
The door hinge left a crack through which I could safely view
And my smile could be hidden so that he never knew

The scene was truly something, it made me smile more
Together with wet footprints, locks of hair lay on the floor
Despite his flaws Tommy still had looked such a hunk
But now he stood there crying, pulling hair out in chunks

You may think it's petty, or childish some would say
But I have to admit that it really made my day
When sadness fills your days and gloominess is rife
Remember to take pleasure in the small things in life...

Josh's Tale

So, I've always liked the ladies, I won't lie to you all
Meeting girls is awesome, as some are really cool
I love that buzz you get when you catch a cutie's eye
And she gives a little smile back, sweet as cherry pie

I love that thrill you feel when you're with somebody new
The touch of unfamiliar hands of a woman (...or two)
Yes, I'm no stranger to multiple entertaining
The odd ménage-a-trios is, quite frankly, good training

I've never had complaints about my sexual prowess
Although unlikely to queue up to inform me, I guess
Still, performance is most commonly measured by result
And I'm frequently moaned at not to halt

I know that that sounds smutty but that's not what I'm about
I'm respectful to a T, not an arrogant lout
Not sexist in the slightest, in fact pretty much from birth
I've been brought up to believe that women run this earth

My mum and dad remain best friends throughout their married life
My dad will often boast about his wonderful wife
Strong and intelligent and loving to the core
A rock for the whole family on which we could all moor

Always there for all of us whatever we went through
Anything we faced, she knew exactly what to do
Mum and Dad have masses of respect for one another
Something that's imparted on myself and my brother

I still like to treat a lady though, ask where she'd like to go
A meal somewhere special, or maybe see a West End show
Buy her nice things, I'm fortunate that I can
I really do appreciate being a wealthy man

I haven't always been – I'm a self-made millionaire!
(...prone to exaggeration, but that's neither here nor there...)
The point is, I enjoy splashing out with what I've earned
You can't take it with you, is one thing that I've learned

I once dated a girl who could have been the real deal
I never will forget the way that she made me feel
She was cute and kind and funny, but here's the thing:
Man could she melt your heart when she started to sing

Just like an angel, her voice could make grown men cry
Whenever she was practicing, it stopped passersby
It wasn't long before she got some really good shows
And started to rake in really good cash, as it goes

She had a local fan base, would turn up at her gigs
I told her she should move out, get herself some new digs
She shared with four others, they were really tight on space
And I knew that she would just adore to have her own place

But she never spent a penny, squirreled it all away
Said the saving up would all be worth it one day
I guess she was still young and that seemed the thing to do
Made more and more money and the savings grew and grew

She'd seen a house she liked, she could afford it as well
But as her stalling increased, her chance to buy it fell
It was everything she wanted – it did my head in
Why she couldn't make her mind up and just kept dithering!

Her indecision won and it got sold in the end
A new search began with the help of her best friend
We had different outlooks, that much was clear to see
I decided that relationship was no longer for me

We went our separate ways, I followed a different path
I had my own ambitions and I don't do things by half
I wanted to commit – throw myself into the throng
But looking back I think that my decision was wrong

Committed to the job – yes, I wanted to go far
Committed to the job – yes, I now own that fancy car
I was young as well. But, I really did love her
I didn't see it *didn't* have to be one or the other

I followed her career with a supportive interest
I'd offered to promote her, bragging that I was the best
Her manager was actually as sound as you can get
So she never switched to me (as she liked a safe bet)

I'll never forget where I was the day the news broke
After a heavy night I was quite jaded when I woke
It had been a good few months since we'd last been in touch
And I'd been so busy that I hadn't thought of her much

The radio sprung to life like an annoying pest
My stupid alarm rudely interrupting my rest
I lay there listening to the news with my eyes still shut
But when they said the victim's name it hit me in the gut

Stalked by a crazy fan who'd taken things too far
Stabbed by this deluded man whilst walking to her car
I thought I would throw up, I just couldn't believe my ears
Stolen from this world, my one true love from all these years

Her best friend told me more on the funeral day
Fitting for our mood, it was miserable and grey
Despite the massive crowd we felt lonely and lost
Reflecting on the terrible price her fame had cost

He'd said "*Hi*" at her gig, followed her Instagram
Commented on every post like some superfan
She'd given in eventually and dated him one night
But he'd come on a bit heavy and he didn't seem right

She'd made it very clear that there'd be no second date
An act that had unfortunately no doubt sealed her fate
He'd grown more obsessed and started to be a pain
And she planned to take it to the police to restrain

Sadly now, too late, but at least he had been caught
Too late for the house and fancy car she never bought
Too late to enjoy the rewards for her skills
...too late to do anything to stop her being killed

Maybe if I'd persevered, I wouldn't have regret?
Maybe if with me, they never would have met?
Could things have turned out differently, turned out right?
Could I have maybe saved her from that fateful night?

There's something to take from this, a lesson to be taught
If you didn't know already: Life is too damn short
This isn't a rehearsal, live your life to the max
'Cos you sure can't take it with you and that's a fact

Jane's Tale

Since I was a young girl, I never had a true friend
Some came close, but no, it's not quite worked out in the end
I like to be by myself, like my own company
I like not relying on others to validate me

When it's only me there's no one else to please
No explaining needed, I can just observe with ease
I haven't got to worry, there's no one to offend
Other people stressing out just drives me round the bend!

I used to sometimes play with the small girl from next door
We were only tiny then, maybe three or four?
Many of the games she liked, well, they weren't really "me"
I mean, who wants to pretend that your teddy bear drinks tea?!

I was often bored, but my mother would insist
Said friendships are important and should not be missed
Crucial for my learning, she was eager that I play
Though I could think of much better ways to spend my day…

…like climbing trees and silently watching passersby…
…like dampening a wing to see if a fly can still fly…
…like seeing how the cat reacts with salt in his cream…
…like noting down the best insects to make my mum scream…

Sometimes it was tea parties, sometimes we'd dress up
Sometimes we would just chase around the garden with her pup
Our "friendship" ended when I accidentally killed a frog
Strangely, I did not see again that girl or her dog

Anyway, that's not the story to be told today
I'll speak of different cruelty (...in a less "explosive" way...)
There are many different ways in which to be unkind
Sticks and stones may break the bones, and fragile is the mind...

As you can imagine I was a loner at school
Never fit with any crowds, the nerdy or the cool
I was often picked on, the brunt of others' fears
Of being deemed inadequate or weak by their peers

Even though I knew the reasons why they'd act this way
It didn't really matter what they'd do or what they'd say
It was always spiteful and it hurt deep down inside
And didn't wash away with tears, despite how much I cried

The school canteen was bad; watch the door to see who'd enter
Weekends were tough too, if I braved the shopping centre
If spotted at the bus stop I'd be made to look a fool
...don't even get me started on my walk home from school

One group in particular would fill my heart with dread
These guys fuelled the fire for the demons in my head
Regarded by many as the coolest gang in town
They did all they could to bring my mood down

The girls could be so cutting, they had a "way" with words
Names the like of which I had never before heard
Where they'd learned these things was beyond my comprehension
The boys would sneer and laugh and were loud, so drew attention

But by far the worst of all, the true bane of my life
The one that hurt the most and caused me the most strife
Their "pack leader"; "alpha male"; call it what you like
The best-looking boy in school: Christopher Turnpike.

I couldn't help but stare at him, his eyes were bright and blue
Hard to think him capable of the things he'd do
His eyes were kind, it led me to believe it's all for show
But then I could never be so cruel, so what do I know?

A bully may be insecure, it could be envy too
They could be suffering themselves but take it out on you
They could just be sadistic and love to see you fall
Knowing reasons why, however, doesn't help at all

Why can't we be resilient? Why can't we just not care?
Why can't our brains just refrain from leading us there?
That dark and lonely place that we go to when we're sad
Dwell in there for too long and you'll end up going mad

I was so preoccupied with amusing myself
That this some way went towards guarding my mental health
The fact I'd read a lot probably helped a bit as well
But that never really stops it from hurting like hell

Sixth Form came and that was a breath of fresh air for me
More space to be invisible, more people to not see
Broader minds, where not everyone sang to the same song
It was so much easier to slip into the throng

Walking out of class one day I spotted on the wall
A poster for the big event – the annual Summer Ball
Regardless of exam results, whether failed or passed
All the local colleges would join to have a blast

Usually, I wouldn't entertain the thought of going
But excitement bubbled within and got my brainwaves flowing
A great opportunity to study behaviour
Now that really was a contemplation I could savour

There'd be a lot of flirting, that went without saying
There'd be those who'd try to blag their way in without paying
There'd be booze and dancing, the band booked were top-notch
And those right off their heads, I could barely wait to watch!

I'd have to buy a dress, of course, I had nothing to wear
I'd have to have a think on what to do about my hair
Then, quite suddenly, it occurred to me
That I could be whoever I decided to be…

This would be fun, I could at last be part of my research
And nobody would know it's me – low risk of besmirch
How would people react if I debriefed them after?...
It could be met with shock, but most likely just laughter

The day arrived – I'd packed it full of hair and nail appointments
Covered head to toe in lotions, masks and ointments
Put in contact lenses and hit the department store
A complimentary make-over, then headed out the door

Strapped some killer heels on (I'd been practicing for weeks!)
Once I'd zipped into my dress I dared to take a peek
The reflection in the mirror… that face and that hair
Even I could not believe it was me standing there

A moment for a pep talk: be brave now and be strong
This was such a good idea, what could possibly go wrong?!
The nerves were creeping up, but I wouldn't let them stay
I took a few deep breaths and the taxi pulled away

My evening progressed well, I was having lots of fun
Blending in and keeping a close eye on everyone
Lots to be observed and lots to jot down in my book
I was so engrossed I'd forgotten how I looked

Taken quite off guard, I felt a hand on my shoulder
I turned and stared into those eyes – the same but now older
Just as bright. Just as blue. I wasn't prepared for this
For standing there in front of me: none other than Chris

So many emotions whizzed around inside of me
Transported back instantly to the girl I used to be
He had no idea of course, why would he, I suppose
Disguised as I was by the hair, make-up and clothes

Spotted me, on my own, from afar, he said
Thought he'd see… offer me a drink and chat instead?
Said that I looked stunning and he'd not seen me around
Took all I could muster to stay put on the ground

Feeling quite light-headed I let him lead the way
Temporarily dumfounded as to what to say
Hadn't he been the one to make my night-times haunted?
But wasn't he truly everything I'd ever wanted?

We hung out with his new friends, danced and had a laugh
Many trips to the bar, he bought on my behalf
The music slowed, he pulled me close – I suddenly felt trapped
I woke up from this daydream and something inside me snapped

He started to get fruity so it came as no surprise
As my hands moved to his waistline and fumbled with his flies
He smiled at me slyly and I smiled back even more
And with one swift movement, his trousers dropped to the floor

Humiliations galore – laughter filled the air
Engulfing us like fire, almost too loud to bear
"Perhaps you'll think of this" I said, as he threw me a glare
"Next time you smear spaghetti hoops into a young girl's hair."

Tony's Tale

My friend Jake would always land himself in hot water
Didn't know when to hold his tongue like he oughta'
I think his mouth ran faster than the speed of his brain
And he'd wind up saying something that he shouldn't, again

Sometimes it was harmless but would still make people grumpy
Like the time he told my mum that her gravy was lumpy
I totally agreed of course, but I'd have never said it
I lived there, after all, I would have lived to regret it!

Sometimes it was funny and would make us all laugh
Like the time he told our Art teacher he needed a bath
Don't get me wrong, Mr Moss stank, he certainly did need it
And although none of us spoke up we all hoped that he'd heed it…

On one occasion it became a little more heated
A big boy had stormed over from where he'd been seated
"*I 'ear you fink I'm stoopid*" he said, ironically
While his gormless friends stood by, rather moronically

One of them gave Jake a shove, I jumped up straight away
But the first boy stepped between us: "*Save it for another day.*
Meet me in the park on Friday, I'll be waiting there.
Bring your friend too, or come alone, if you dare."

And so, we braved the park (…with Jake *slightly* behind me….)
Ambushed by these kids, who dropped down from a tree
I've always been quick though and nimble on my feet
With a few swift manoeuvres they would soon regret this meet

Quite intimidating: they were all larger than me
But I've always been quite fearless, don't see what others see
A lion in the middle, a troll stood either side
I simply saw three boys with nowhere now to hide

The main boy had held back, pushed his puppets to the fore
I ducked from their big lunges and they both fell to the floor
They were both so slow it was easy to spin round
Pulled their tops over their heads to keep them on the ground

The main kid then stepped forward but was being a bit slow
I guess that his two heavies usually dealt out the blows
I jumped on his bewilderment and used nature's tools
Snagged him by his hood against a tree, like a fool

Once there was no danger, Jake clapped his hands and cheered
We turned and walked away from those boys he had feared
Merrily he skipped around, excited by this "win"
Called me his hero, for bravely protecting him

All the way home he relayed details of the fight
Exaggerating everything of course, like you might
The fight had lasted hours, by the time we parted
(and not, in fact, been over before it had even started):

The goons had butted heads and been covered in mud:
The main boy was left crying and covered in blood:
I'd taken a few punches… it was all *much* gorier
Jake made me out to be like some great orc warrior

I didn't mind, it felt nice to have done something good
To have stuck it to the bullies and for all that they stood
I hated the injustice; Jake was only a squirt
And although he said daft things, didn't deserve to get hurt

Some time passed us by without much going on
No repercussions, no canary's song
They seemed to avoid us and we avoided them
But a few months down the road saw Jake in trouble again

We were due to meet to kick a ball about
There must be something up, of that I had no doubt
Jake was rarely late and never a no-show
I waited for an hour before deciding to go

I went round to his house and he looked like he'd been crying
I asked him what was up and that there was no point lying
I told him to be straight and tell me what was going on
But he answered in a whisper that there was nothing wrong

I waited for a few days but questioned him again
Thought that he might need the support of a good friend
He told me he'd been jumped while walking home from the store
They'd taken all his money and kicked him to the floor

I was fuming. Who'd done this?! Why hadn't he told me?
Was it that same boy who I'd left hooked to the tree?
He'd been alone – no sidekicks – no one around to see
I quickly racked my brains as to where about he'd be….

As it was the weekend it was pretty hard to know
But there were one or two places I knew he liked to go
I tried the park; the arcade; my resolve running deep
Even the shop that sold out-of-date crisps off really cheap

I was out all day and I was tired on my feet
When who should I clap eyes on just walking down the street
The very sight of him was making my blood boil
His plans to bully once again, I knew I had to spoil

I ran across that road and with the full weight of my fist
I planted my right hook, there was no way I'd have missed
At first a yell of pain followed by a loud thud
As he dropped to the floor like an old sack of spuds

"*That's for Jake*" I said, "*now leave him the hell alone*"
I turned and started walking, I just wanted to get home
He called out after me, said he hadn't got a clue
He thought this thing between us had been well and truly through?

That just made me angry, as I had thought the same
The fact he'd kicked things off again had made him fair game
I said that jumping Jake alone had been the final straw
Of course he would protest, I'd expected nothing more

He was really adamant that I had got things wrong
Said that Jake had been the troublemaker all along
Said I should think wisely before choosing my friends
In case they turned out not to be so nice, in the end

I brushed off what he said back then, I didn't much care
Thought him just a big bully and full of hot air
Jake thought he was stupid and "not right in the head"
Why on earth would I listen to anything he said?

Fast forward a few months and my peg would be knocked down
I was playing football on the other side of town
A "friendly" at another school, I'd not been there before
Spotted it as soon as I walked through the sports hall door…

A photo of the bully; right there for all to see
A beaming grin across his face, as wide as it could be
It said he was the champion and pictured next to him
Was a pupil from this school who'd just missed out on the win

I stopped to read some more and couldn't believe my eyes
It seems that chess was his game, at which he'd won his prize
But how could that be so? Didn't you have to be bright
To be any good at chess and win that checkerboard fight?

Jake said he was stupid and so I'd assumed he knew
Taken everything my friend had said to be true
As I continued reading there was more to digest
It suddenly dawned on me: the date of the contest

Saturday the 21st – that rang a bell for sure
The date that Jake was "jumped" while walking home from the store…
Or so he had told me and I'd believed him, just like that
A realisation dawned that I had been, in fact, a prat…

I didn't want to think that my friend had lied to me
But the facts spoke for themselves, there was no way it could be
The date and times conflicted, it just wasn't legit.
And I was left confused, feeling like a prize twit

I'd jumped to conclusions, taken lies spoken as true
Something there and then I vowed never again to do
Events would have been different if only I'd have known
Things seen from another's eyes don't always match our own

Without the full picture it's easy to make mistakes
Before acting impulsively, I should put on the brakes
I would now endeavour to do this, hopefully
As I saw I had unwittingly become the bully

It turned out Jake had simply been told off by his folks
He'd lied to me to save face and as a sort of "joke"
It would be too easy to lay all the blame on him
But of course, in truth, Jake hadn't made me do a single thing

Kel's Tale

I used to see my cousins quite a lot when we were young
They weren't poor like us, their toys were always so much fun
Thomo had a nerf gun, we would play with it all day
From dawn to dusk, until the dark had chased the sun away

He also had real Lego, not the kind that poorly fit
So when we'd finished building, it didn't look all shit!
But my favourite were their rollerblades: man, were they cool
I would shoot round there to play with him straight after school

His sister May was tiny but she had a big bite
She'd never let me borrow hers, purely out of spite
She didn't care for hers, plus we had the same size feet
And me and Thomo wanted to go up and down the street

Taking turns with Thomo's pair just wasn't the same
Both wearing blades opened up so many more games
We snuck up to her room while she was round her friend's
But she'd hidden them from us! It drove us round the bend

We had a good old rummage, then looked under the bed
Nowhere to be found, but we found something else instead
May's favourite toy sat pride of place up on the shelf
I had this great idea (even if I say so myself)

She loved her "Girl's World", although we thought that it looked odd
The thing nightmares are made of: a head without a bod
I fetched the kitchen scissors and gave Thomo a wink
Then I cut off all its hair and washed it down the sink

"WHERE'S HER HAIR?!!!!!!" I never will forget her shouting out
We thought it was so funny, even though we got a clout
Her mum tried to help matters by painting on some hair
And looking at that pretty face, I couldn't help but stare…

Something in the way the eyes drew all of your attention
Without hair to distract, there was so much more to mention
Her lips and cheekbones stood out, she didn't have a flaw
The doll looked better now, I thought, than ever before

Back then it was a fleeting thought, I dwelt on it no more
Years later, as a teenager, when Shaznay I first saw
That memory popped into my head, a vision to behold
With her hair slicked back so tight, it looked like she was bald

But her eyes twinkled brightly, she's got such a pretty face
When I laid eyes on her it knocked all others out the race
We were at the local lido, all mucking about
When my mate started pointing and said "*'ere, check this out!*"

Shaznay and her girlfriends had been in the pool swimming
They were only girls, trying hard to look like women
We thought they looked well fit, so we didn't really care
With full faces of makeup and scanty cut swimwear

She'd sunbathe at the lido and I'd gawk from afar
She was aloof and giggly, as girls her age are
I never thought she'd notice me, much less give a snog
But that's exactly what happened to this lucky dog

The boys had played a joke on me, but it had backfired
We'd been swimming all day and I was really tired
I'd nodded off – sound asleep – in the scorching sun
So the boys had decided to have a bit of fun…

Now, I've got such fair skin that I burn up good and proper
I simply go bright red, none of this "sun-kissed copper"
I usually cover up, wear a cap on my head
But that day I hadn't, I was so tired, like I said

My mates had taken pebbles and lined them all up tight
I didn't feel them on me, I was out like a light
So smug: they thought they were so clever, real cutting edge…
But yes, you've guessed the shape they went for: meat and two veg….

When I woke and sat up the pebbles fell to the floor
They all rolled about laughing and praised themselves some more
I laughed along with them, but not really in the know
That wouldn't be apparent until we went to go…

As I headed over towards the changing room gates
I had to walk right past Shaznay and all of her mates
She stared at me and smiled: well, I nearly dropped down dead!
Then she shouted "*'ere, why've you got a nob on your forehead?!*"

I wished the floor would open up and swallow me deep
This was pretty low for even my friends to steep
So embarrassed, I couldn't get away quick enough
But to make things worse I tripped, dropping all of my stuff

Eventually I made it into the shower block
Feeling crap, my confidence had taken a right knock
I looked into the metal mirror screwed to the wall
And saw my mates' handiwork – at least it was quite small

Feeling quite dejected, I got into the shower
It felt like I was standing there for hours and hours
I was on a go-slow, no attention to the clock
But when I went to get dressed, I was in for a shock

My shorts were gone! Oh man, this couldn't be any worse
That day just made me feel like I was under a curse
I'd have to venture out to see if the coast was clear
Otherwise I'd end up spending all night long in here

I poked my head outside and scanned the place, left and right
Everyone had cleared off and there was no one in sight
"*At last*" I thought, "*finally some luck has come my way!*"
The clouds had come and turned that scorching sky dark and grey

I ran towards the exit, thankful for the weather
Then BAM! There was Shaznay getting her things together
She eyed me up and down and decided to be blunt
But she smiled first, and winked, saying "*I like your Y-fronts…*"

As we walked home together we laughed about my day
We had a lot in common and got on straight away
She'd lent me some spare joggers, and then I met her mum
Not ideal, 'cos they had "JUICY" written on the bum…

Luckily she'd had some make-up too, to sort my head
Or else the thought of her place would have filled me with dread
But Shaznay's mum is sound and we all wondered at my shorts
Even now, exactly what occurred still enters my thoughts

I'm guessing that it was the boys, but they never said
Surprised, if they did it, they'd plead ignorance instead
More likely, they'd take credit and find themselves well funny
Gutted though: I loved those shorts, what a waste of money

So, little did they know when they tried to stitch me up
That I'd be the one victorious, lifting the cup
My mates cannot believe that we are getting it on
So, in one respect, at least, I always feel like The Don

Shaznay's Tale

I should probably start by saying I grew up in Wales
By way of explanation, before you judge these tales
There's really not that much to do for curious girls
Once you've tired of dressing up in mum's heels and fake pearls

I discovered snogging at a very young age
Too early, some would say, but that's pretty hard to gauge
When nothing's going on you have to make your own fun
And girls plus boys, equals intrigue, when all's said and done

We'd practiced on ourselves at first, the back of our hand
But that was really boring and seemed a little bland
We then progressed to where your forefinger meets your thumb
You know, that little hole that's formed, where you can poke your tongue

After that we'd had enough, wanted to try for real
Have a boy in front of us and how his mouth would feel
The boys were up for it of course, most were fairly game
And though it felt naughty it was really rather tame

By the end of that term, I'd snogged the boys in my class
All of them except for Aled, who opted to pass
Back then we hadn't realised, we were too young to see
That I think Aled had secretly wished that he were me

I'd even cornered Thomas who was the class bookworm
That had been well funny, I'd enjoyed watching him squirm
A smooch on the lips was a bit too much for some
Who'd only known a quick peck on the cheek from their mum

I continued to want more, the thrill of something new
Some boys were willing, although we didn't have a clue
A tickle here; a fondle there; most of it was nice
Except when I played with dirty Dave and ended up with lice

The Youth Club held a disco, we would all get dolled up
Put makeup on and stuff socks in to fill our "B" cups
It was our chance to hang out and get up to no good
And get off with boys of course, if we said that they could

I experimented, keen to keep trying new things
Eager for excitement and what each new month would bring
Sometimes my BFs were shocked when I said what I'd done
We'd giggle though, knowing it was just a bit of fun

This one time I met a boy travelling with the fair
It meant that he'd be gone in weeks, but we didn't care
He was sweet and funny and so different to the rest
Just looking at his dark eyes made me want to get undressed

His accent was unusual, which magnified the charm
And not being from Wales didn't do any harm!
He'd travelled the whole country, from Cornwall to Dundee
And learned a few things which he could certainly teach me

He could make me feel things that I'd never felt before
Take me to new heights without leaving the trailer floor
Although he had big, strong hands, he had a soft caress
And half hour alone with him would get me in a mess

Speaking of which, brings me to my story I will share
For it involves my fairground boy, while he was still there
We didn't have that long together, but it was fun
And had things been different, maybe away with him I'd have run

Don't get me wrong, I love my Kel and I feel I should say
That I don't secretly wish things had been a different way….
But I'm glad for knowing him and that, that night we met
And certainly, this night in question, I'll never forget

It was a sunny afternoon, we'd been to the woods
We'd fooled around under the trees, just because we could
The sky was blue, a warm wind and the song of the leaves
As they danced with the shadows, all in tune with the breeze

It was one of those summer days that just make you smile
That make you simply want to laze around for a while
Do absolutely nothing, even though you really should
The kind of day you wish you could hold on to, for good

Possibly I put it down to such a perfect day
But things went a little far… in fact, all the way
We still had our clothes on, only half-hoicked here and there
Because although secluded, I had still been a bit scared

It wasn't really everything I'd hoped it would be
Much more "Antiques Roadshow" and a lot less "MTV"
It felt pretty awkward and was all over so quick
And I'd probably need a Tetanus for a gouge from a stick

After, when the deed was done, we lay there for a bit
I stared up at the sky, feeling a bit of a tit
Had I been any good? Oh no, had I been gurning?!
I know I'd squirmed right as he reached the point of no returning

I pulled my skirt back down and he straightened up his shorts
A million and one things were racing through my thoughts
He hadn't said a word, but he now looked with disdain
At the groin region of his shorts, and an unpleasant stain

I told him not to worry, for I never went out
Without being prepared (I should have been a boy scout!)
"…just grab a wet wipe from my bag and give it a rub
It will be fine by later, when we go to the club"

I used it when he'd finished, as I noticed my skirt
Had also fallen victim to the wrath of his squirt
At least my skirt and his shorts were both white as snow
So by the time they'd dried it would hardly even show

For disco night it was and we were heading straight there
We thought that it would make a nice change from the fair
And even though soon, he would no longer be around
I wanted to show off this well-fit boy that I'd found

My girlfriends would be green, I could see their faces now
And even though it made me a bit of a cow
The local lads could do with seeing they should up their game
'Cause when the fair left town, they'd have to do, once again

It wouldn't hurt for them to pull their socks up a tad
Make a bit more effort and be nicer, like this lad
Not everything has to be about joking with friends
Didn't they see it would be worth their while, in the end

The youth club hall was packed and we danced for all to see
It was quite unusual for a boy to impress me
He certainly could move, he had rhythm running free
I would have danced all night, but I had to take a pee!

We made our way across the hall, through the crowded floor
The light was a shocker, outside in the corridor
Everyone milling around, waiting for the loos
I was buzzing, but then I started to feel confused

Lots of people staring, and giggling behind hands
Whispering and smirking, not at all how I had planned
I thought we looked good together, oozing confidence
Until I heard, those haunting words: "*eeeeurgh, you've shat your pants!*"

I looked to where they pointed and much to my dismay
Brown marks now covered our clothes, from earlier that day
A sudden realisation came flooding to my head
He'd only gone and grabbed one of my tanning wipes instead!

He couldn't forgive me for making him look daft
All my friends and other kids had just stood there and laughed
There seemed little point in arguing who was to blame
As he walked out of my life for good that night – such a shame.

Sofe's Tale

I miss my nanny Josephine, we did so much together
Always memories to be made, whatever the weather
She made me look at everything in a different way
She made me laugh at something new, every single day

In the sun we'd lay in grass, that swayed high all around us
Pretending we were sleeping lions, no one would have found us
When it rained we'd build a den, with sheets and boxes galore
Or make our way around a room without touching the floor

One day we went into town to buy Mother a present
Spring was in the air and the temperature was pleasant
Mother's Day was fast approaching (I'd handmade a card)
When unexpectedly it rained, catching us off guard

Josephine thought quickly, as she hadn't brought my coat
"*I'll sort this in a flash*" she said and then cleared her throat
With a rip here and some knots there, I was dry as a bone
With a cape fit for a princess, sat atop her throne

But this princess did not sit, no! I skipped joyfully
With my multicoloured cape on, which filled me with glee
I floated like a butterfly, all the while keeping dry
And rustled like the wind up high, swirling leaves into the sky

Along the country lanes and through the meadows we ran
All the while laughing, all the while hand in hand
I felt safe with Josephine wherever we were
There was something warm and comforting about her

She wasn't very old, but she wasn't very young
Her voice spoke everything as if it should be sung
Her eyes seemed to smile, even though her mouth was flat
And she had bouncy hair, but wore it back in a plait

Luckily for us Mother was out when we returned
For my splendid cape was not so splendid after all, I learned
Father laughed, but pointed out that one was not to brag
When dancing round in a mish-mash of carrier bags

He could see the fun in things: Mother sadly, not so
She would have been mad in case the neighbours saw my show
I was always careful to behave just as I should
I didn't want to be naughty; I strived to be good

But I had heard raised voices on occasion, got too near
Behind closed doors when probably they thought no one could hear
I would run off to my room and try hard not to cry
Repeat my numbers out loud: "*un, deux, trois…*", "*…eins, zwei, drei…*"

I hated thinking of my parents as being sad
I really hoped it wasn't me making them so mad
I tried my best to please; did everything asked of me
All I wanted was to be a happy family

One year for my birthday Josephine planned a surprise
She led me to the garden, whilst covering my eyes
There, to my amazement, all sat in the Autumn sun
Were all my favourite friends! "*Now*", she said, "*time for fun*!"

The table had been set with pretty teacups and plates
And bunting hung around, just like at the Summer Fete
I had my fill of cupcakes and cookies and milk
Then Josephine spun me round, my eyes covered with silk

"*Make sure you count to 50, before you come to seek!
…and no lifting up the scarf; you simply mustn't peek!*"
We also played a game of "Simon Says" and "I Spy"
And made shapes out of the clouds that passed by in the sky

That afternoon was lovely, I remember it well
The colour of the cupcakes and even their sweet smell
The smiles and the laughter surrounded by my friends
I loved that day so much that I wished it wouldn't end

Soon enough Mother appeared to call me back indoors
I had piano practice and Josephine, some chores
I didn't want to go; I was having so much fun
I must admit, I stropped a bit, starting with "...*but MUUUUM?????*

*...It nearly is my birthday and all my friends are here
Couldn't we have one more hour? Why don't you join the cheer?*"
Mother then looked from Patch to Anna, Barney to Ted
A sadness filled her eyes and she slowly shook her head

"*Come inside please. Leave your toys, I'll tidy them later*"
Right there in that moment, I really did hate her
Well, not true hate of course, just the tantrum of a child
And perhaps the first inkling of being a bit wild...

I hadn't many friends and no sisters or brothers
Not Father's decision; most definitely Mother's
Father would joke he would have liked a whole football team
But soon things were to change for us and shatter that dream

A rainy afternoon in my wellies and raincoat
We sailed off down the garden in a magnificent boat
Josephine had fashioned a most glorious vessel
From an old shower curtain and half of an old trestle

We bobbed among the hedges at the end of the lawn
And I learned about the fairies who played there at dawn
Josephine knew all their names and their favourite flowers
I could have listened to her stories for hours and hours

It was nearly teatime when the sky began to clear
Josephine leaned in to me and whispered in my ear
"*I'll share with you a secret, if you promise not to tell
I'm not just your nanny*" she said, "*but your fairy godmother as well*"

With my eyes full of wonder, she granted me a wish
I had to think about it; didn't want to be selfish
I had all that I needed; couldn't ask for any more
My eyes then settled on a window, on the second floor

Merely silhouettes but it was obvious to see
Arguing again, hands waving animatedly
I knew right there and then what my wish should surely be
I wanted us to be, once more, a happy family

"*I want them to be happy please, that's what I wish for
Anger be gone from this house and arguments, no more*"
Josephine slowly nodded, then rose from where she knelt
A strange sense came over me, like never before felt

She looked up at the house with a deep look in her eyes
A rainbow had appeared bursting right across the sky
The wind picked up her loose curls and they danced in the breeze
She turned and smiled down at me and gave my hand a squeeze

That day was a turning point, but not how I had thought
The next day mother disappeared and a divorce she sought
My father, although empty, seemed much more at peace
And certainly, one thing's for sure, the arguments did cease

The guilt sometimes consumes me, it's as though my brain's been burnt
And I scream at my naivety and what I've since learnt
That one person's "happy" may be "sad" for the other
And so, they turned down different paths, my father and mother

Be careful what you wish for as it may just come true
And it may not play out the way you thought it would do
No matter how improbable, it *may* have been my fault
And I'll carry that forever in my memory vault

Oliver's Tale

My dad had skipped out on us when I was barely three
Didn't want to be there for either my mum or me
She rarely spoke about him, mainly when she was mad
And cross at me for something, whenever I'd been bad

Fortunately, I was quite the well-behaved child
So her tickings-off were short lived and reasonably mild
She stated that I got my belligerence from Dad
And had a way of arguing the same as he had

Essentially, I had to be, all of the time right
Stubbornness and silence were my way to win the fight
Little did my mum know what went on inside my head
That in truth, I was struggling for the right words to be said

It wasn't that I didn't want to talk these things through
My mouth just wouldn't say what my brain wanted it to
Frustration adding to the feelings I could not express
When I tried to speak my mind, I'd get in a mess

But that was all to change after wise words from a friend
When given the right tools, it's much easier to mend
"*Take your time. Breathe. Try to describe your thoughts instead.
Use simple words when you get stuck*" is what Percy said

Percy came into my life when I needed it most
"*Here, Son*" he'd piped up, whilst leaning on our garden post
"*You're catching that ball wrong – you need to draw your arms in*"
And just like that our father-son-like bond would begin

He taught me how to ride a bike with no balance wheels
He taught me how to run better, without heavy heels
He taught me to be grateful for all of Mum's meals
And he taught me that whatever hurts, only time heals

I love my mum dearly but she had to work each day
There was little time for her to teach me things or play
I helped her with the housework, not that we made much mess
And the fact I kept myself amused caused her less stress

I'd often chat to Percy about problems at school
I'd had to talk in class and wound up looking a fool
Percy had been keen to give me advice if he could
And those words he'd said to me, did me the world of good

Not only were they helpful but they left me inspired
Learning words became something of which I never tired
I could sit and devour the dictionary for hours
And I learnt that speaking well brought with it certain powers

I fell in love with Eve when I was only seven
Her face was so angelic, like she'd come from heaven
She was smart and funny and not interested in boys
I mean, we were just seven, it was all about toys!

But Percy said to me I should perhaps write her a rhyme
And tell her I thought of her from sunrise to bedtime
I tried but I must admit, I found it hard going
To put my heart out there, with all my feelings showing

So instead, I wrote of her and praised her for a while
But the rest was intended simply to make her smile
Luckily it paid off and she thought me rather clever
And we spent all of that summer playing happily together

Percy one day asked me if I knew much of my dad
I was honest with him and it made him really sad
We talked for a long time about my thoughts on it all
Until the sun went down and the night began to fall

I hadn't known my dad enough to "grieve", as it were
I'd been so young that memories were mostly a blur
I wouldn't know his face, but for the photos mum kept
But the way he broke her heart I could never accept

Percy couldn't understand how any man could choose
To walk out on their wife and kid, with so much to lose
He said he'd had a son himself, a long time before
And spending time with me was helping mend his heart more

"Taken far too young - such a waste of life", he sighed
I knew from prior talks that his wife had also died
I realised that we all will lose someone we adore
And when that time arrived for me, I'd hurt even more

I wanted him to know how much he meant to me too
To have a father figure, to show me what to do
To teach me crucial lessons on how we all should live
It was the greatest gift he could possibly give

I told him I was thankful for all he had taught me
For all the free-falling moments, when he had caught me
For times when I had needed picking up off the floor
But teaching me to help myself had meant so much more

One day we decided to tackle my biggest fear
The boarded-up basement door that I'd never go near
It always creeped me out, so away from it I'd stayed
But enough was enough – I was tired of being afraid

I undid some screws and then removed the planks of wood
Studying the keyhole, as in front of it I stood
Remembered that the kitchen dresser had a junk drawer
Full of keys, which soon lay strewn across the kitchen floor

I must have tried most, until eventually I found
A big, old, rusty mortise key lying on the ground
It turned with a mighty clunk – the hinge gave a creak
As the door swung wide open, I was too scared to speak

We ventured down the stairs; it was dark and it was cold
There was a smell in the air, you simply know as "old"
I started to panic, a familiar feeling
But luckily a bare lightbulb hung from the ceiling

With a flick of the old switch a dim light was released
As the shadows chased away, my bravery increased
The basement was enormous and filled with mostly junk
But over in one corner I spotted a large trunk

It opened with a groan and I thought that I might faint
To not slam that lid down again took me some restraint
Atop, a silver box that was no longer shiny
And two human skeletons – one larger and one tiny

The little box was filled with loose newspaper cuttings
And an old, faded photograph, out of those was jutting
Reports of a local man, a hero killed at war
And the image was this man, who before me I saw

Here his wife and child lay – both their lives she'd taken
Put to bed one final time, never to awaken
The never-ending torment of the husband she'd lost
With her sanity paying the ultimate cost

Percy had just wanted the truth to be uncovered
He seemed at peace now that these things I had discovered
He smiled kindly and a bright light behind him shone
I only blinked my eyes and just like that, he was gone

Of course, as I'd grown older, I'd realised it was queer
That no one looked at Percy whenever he was here
I'd never heard anyone else ever speak his name
And even though time passed by, he always looked the same

Perhaps deep down I knew but had never been daunted
By the prospect of living in a house that was haunted
My mum had often exclaimed *"who' you talking to love?"*
I know now our friendship was forged by powers above.

Close

So, there you have it, all the tales – be they true or false
Then came the task of choosing the winner, of course
But time flies and before they knew it, they had arrived
Eager to part ways and party; not keen to decide

Possibly because they saw merit in them all
And each so different, it would be a real tough one to call
If a crown was given it would have been done in haste
As they were keen to start the festivities they faced

But we can assume that they all had formed a bond
Whether or not of one another they were fond
Some would stay in touch; some would stay ships in the night
For some, it may have been cathartic, as you'd think it might

Everyone had opened up, or woven a tall tale
But with, perhaps, a thread of truth, so insight would prevail
All had learned something of their travellers akin
Making it a weighty task, deciding who should win

But, alas, we'll never know, it's been lost over time
(Perhaps because it was never recorded in rhyme…)
Something which, no doubt, will be looked on with regret
For if things are not passed along, we're quick to forget.

Epilogue

That which I can tell you is repeated now, herewith
A hint at the "what became of...?"s, is all I give
For when one's busy partying, try hard as you might
The last thing on your mind is picking up a pen to write

For big brother Tony, it opened up his eyes
To learn that Jane was bullied had come as a surprise
She had never let on, or spoken out at home
And it saddened him that she had gone through it alone

He felt a pang of guilt when thinking how he had been
Though it had never been his intention to be mean
He wanted Jane to know that he would always be there
And that they should be closer, as he really did care

Jane was in agreement, as she loved Tony dearly
But now was not the time, for she was focused clearly
On another of their party, who had caught her eye
To her, Oliver, seemed a hell of a guy!

So articulate, she loved observing him speak
And so sexy too (a bonus!), it made her knees weak
A mutual attraction, they planned a rendezvous
To take in all on offer and do all they could do

Oliver was overjoyed, Jane had got him hooked
Intelligent. Witty. And her beauty overlooked
She had lovely features, though behind her specs she hid
He wanted to undo the damage the bullying did

Josh's wish came true in that he found his new star act
This duo could be something big and cause quite an impact
Very different each, but when together they sang
It sounded so pure, that on each single word you'd hang

Sandie's voice was soft; clear, but blurry round the edges
Sophia's voice was husky; much more Benson and Hedges
They complimented one another, who would have known
But for joining in a sing-song on that bus, far from home

They struck up a close friendship, this unlikely pair
And each of them could see there was something more there
They found a comfort in each other, safety and calm
And happiness beyond compare in each other's arms

As for Bro and Suzie, well, they'd seen it all before
Year on year they had a blast, enjoyed it even more
Those fields were like a second home, come rain or come shine
Always it was an awesome trip and always blew their minds

They'd live out their lives together, they'd both seen a lot
Thankful for some peace now, thankful for what they'd got
They both appreciated the small pleasures life can bring
So why not enjoy together and share in everything

Finally, our two Welsh youngsters …there we're not so sure
Shaznay was last spotted crawling around on all fours
She hadn't dropped an earring; those hoops you'd spot real quick
But maybe something else was dropped and now she felt sick

And as the camera pans out for our final bird's-eye view
We linger very briefly on the last of our few
Kel was raving wildly, with a glow stick in his hand
And the biggest smile across his face, lighting up the land.

Acknowledgements

The biggest thanks to my wonderful Steve (Shteeeeeve). Without your encouragement, help and generosity I would never have pulled my socks up and finished this.

To Debs and Vic for your suggestions and enthusiasm.

To my mum and my Auntie Eileen, and their letters back and forth, written entirely in rhyme.

To my sister, for telling me to just write how you speak.

... and to my dad, for uttering those five seemingly small words to me many, many moons ago: "you should write a book"...

...and Apologies

...for dropping in "for sikerly" – I couldn't resist a little nod to old Geoff. If you haven't looked it up already, it means "definitely/surely/certainly" (take your pick)

All errors are entirely mine.

This is a pure work of fiction, straight from my noggin. If any similarities to actual persons, or actual events, cause upset or offence, I am truly sorry.

This book won't be for everyone. ...ahh well, you win some, you lose some...

Thank you for reading.

About the Author

Jo was born and raised in Essex, but now resides on the beautiful south coast of Dorset.

In her spare time she can usually be found strolling through sand, fields or forest with her husband and dog.

Although Jo's produced many scribblings over the years, The Glastonbury Tales is her first novella.